Coventry Public Library

S0-BYN-326

3 2224 00257 8456

COVENTRY PUBLIC LIBRARY

COVENTRY PUBLIC LIBRARY

Mother's Day
Surprise

by
Stephen Krensky

illustrated by
Kathi Ember

two lions

two lions

Text copyright © 2010 by Stephen Krensky
Illustrations copyright © 2010 by Kathi Ember
All rights reserved
Amazon Publishing
Attn: Amazon Children's Publishing
P.O. Box 400818, Las Vegas, NV 89140
www.amazon.com/amazonchildrenspublishing

Library of Congress Cataloging-in-Publication Data

Krensky, Stephen.
  Mother's Day surprise / by Stephen Krensky ; illustrated by
Kathi Ember. — 1st ed.
      p. cm.
  Summary: After watching the other animals make Mother's
Day gifts, Violet the snake tries hard to think of something
nice that she can make for her mother.
  ISBN 9781477810521
  [1. Mother's Day—Fiction. 2. Gifts—Fiction. 3. Snakes—
Fiction. 4. Animals—Fiction.] I. Ember, Kathi, ill. II. Title.
PZ7.K883Mo 2010
[E]—dc22   2009006320

The illustrations are rendered in acrylics.
Book design by Vera Soki
Editor: Margery Cuyler
Printed in China

For my mother
—S.K.

To my mom, Theresa,
for her endless love and support
—K.E.

Violet was a young snake.
She liked sliding and slithering and shedding her skin whenever it got old.

In her free time, Violet often
played with the other animals.
She raced the rabbits.

She hung next to the bats.

And she fooled around with the chipmunks.

But as spring was sprung, Violet noticed a change in the air. The other animals were suddenly very busy. Too busy to play.

Violet wondered why everyone was in such a hurry.
"What's the rush?" she asked a fox trotting by.
"Things to do," he said
Violet could see that. "What things?" she asked.
But the fox was already gone.

Violet looked around for anyone with a moment to spare.
"What's going on?" she asked a skunk digging in the dirt.
"We're getting ready for Mother's Day," he explained.
"Already?" said Violet.
The skunk laughed. "Well, you can't start too soon.
It takes time to make the perfect gift."
Violet had to admit that was true.
But what kind of gift would be perfect for *her* mother?

Violet watched a squirrel sorting through
a pile of acorns.
He was very picky about it.
"Why are you being so fussy?" Violet asked.
"They're for my mother," said the squirrel.
"And she likes them crunchy."

Next, Violet saw a bear crushing some honeycombs.
"That looks like sticky work," said Violet.
The bear agreed. "But I have to do it right.
My mother likes things just so."

Then Violet saw a beaver chomping on a fallen tree trunk.
"What are you doing?" Violet asked.
"Shhhhh!" said the beaver. "Don't disturb the artist at work."
"Sorry," said Violet.
"I can't afford to make any mistakes," the beaver went on.
"When I'm done, my mother will love this."

Violet was glad everyone was working so hard.
But that wasn't helping her.
What could she do for her own mother?
Without arms or legs or teeth, she couldn't
make anything like the other animals.

Never before had Violet felt it was hard being a snake.
But she felt that way now.

As Mother's Day approached, Violet got sadder
and sadder. The other animals were finishing up
their gifts. And Violet still hadn't started hers.
It wasn't fair. It wasn't fair at all.

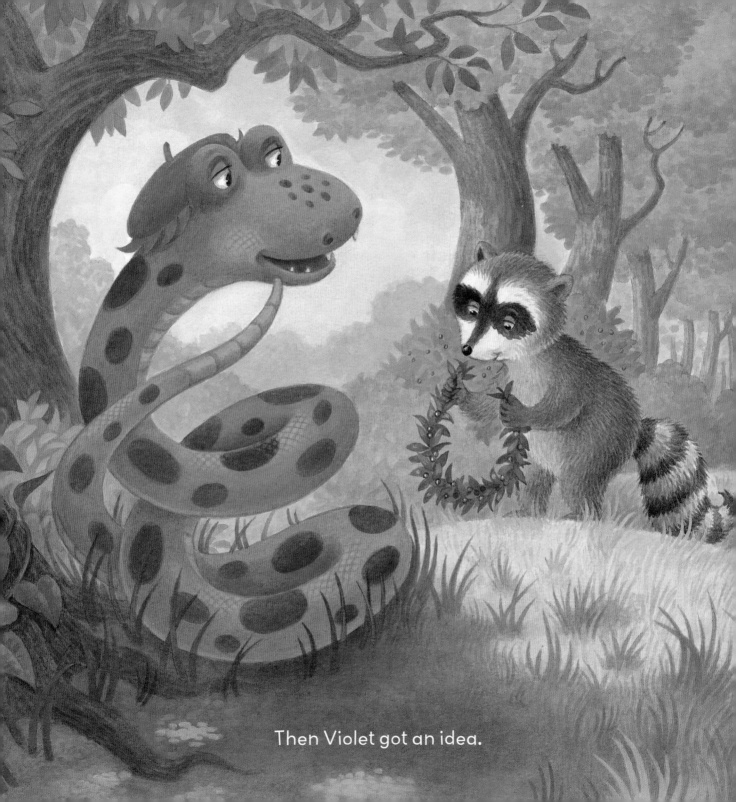

Then Violet got an idea.

She practiced and practiced
her present in secret.

It was a tricky business.

But slowly she made progress.

On the morning of Mother's Day,
all the animals were ready with their presents.

Violet was ready, too.

"HAPPY MOTHER'S DAY!" shouted Violet.
"Oh, my," said her mother. "What a nice surprise!
It's perfect, Violet. Absolutely perfect."

Violet was very happy.
Even without arms or legs or teeth,
she had shown her mother just how she felt.

And her mother felt
the same way, too.

COVENTRY PUBLIC LIBRARY